MASHED POTATO MOUNTAIN

ISBN 0-88753-156-3

Published in January 1988 by Black Moss Press,
1939 Alsace St., Windsor, Ontario N8W 1M5.
Financial assistance toward this publication was
provided by the Canada Council and the Ontario
Arts Council.

Black Moss books are distributed in Canada and the
U.S. by Firefly Books, 250 Sparks Avenue,
Willowdale, Ontario, Canada M2H 2S4.
All orders should be directed there.

MASHED POTATO MOUNTAIN

Written by Laurel Dee Gugler
Illustrated by Leonard Aguanno

Black Moss Press
1988

"What's for dinner?" asked Jamie.

"Mashed potatoes, gravy, vegetables and fresh bread," said Mom.

"Yummy, I love mashed potatoes," said Jamie.

He took a huge blob of mashed potatoes. He made a mountain.

"Eat your mashed potatoes," said Mom.

"I can't eat a mountain!" said Jamie.

"No, I guess you can't," agreed Mom.

Jamie made part of the mountain flat.

Then he dug some pools. He filled the pools with gravy. He dug a river between the pools. He watched the muddy gravy water flow between. He dug a lake on top of the mountain.

Then he made a waterfall.
SWOOOSH!
Down came the gravy
water into the river.

"Do you like your gravy?" asked Mom.

"I can't eat a river," said Jamie.

"No, I guess you can't," said Mom.

Jamie planted some bushes.

He planted some trees.

He planted a whole forest.

"Have you eaten your vegetables?" asked Mom.

"I can't eat a forest," said Jamie.

"No, I guess you can't," sighed Mom.

Jamie cut a strip of bread. He made a bridge.

"The bread is fresh. Have you tasted it?" asked Mom.

"Oh Mom, I can't eat a bridge!" said Jamie.

"No, you definitely can't eat a bridge," agreed Mom. Then she went to the freezer and took something out. "Guess what's for dessert," she said.

"Oooh," said Jamie,
"monsters can eat bridges.
Monsters can eat anything.
I'm a monster."

He ate the bridge …

and the river …

and the
mountain ...

"Now, may I have ice cream?" he asked.

"You can't eat a snowman!" said Mom.

"A MONSTER CAN!" growled Jamie.